DISCARD

Try Your Best

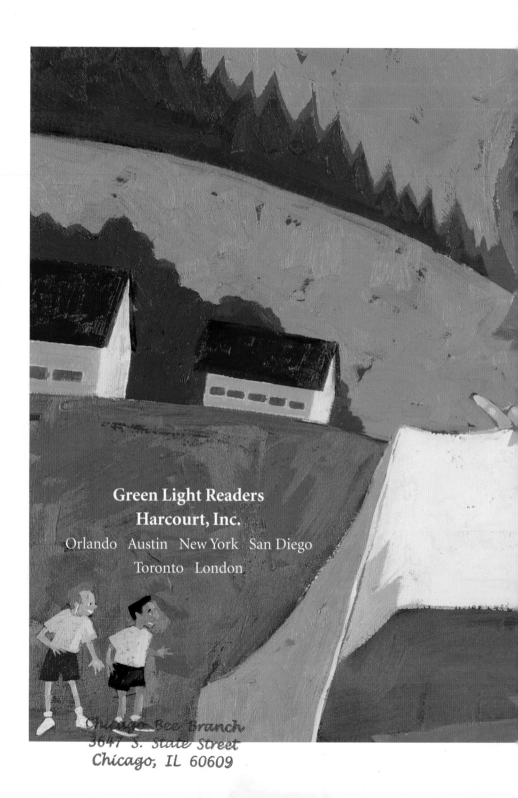

Green Light Readers
Harcourt, Inc.
Orlando Austin New York San Diego
Toronto London

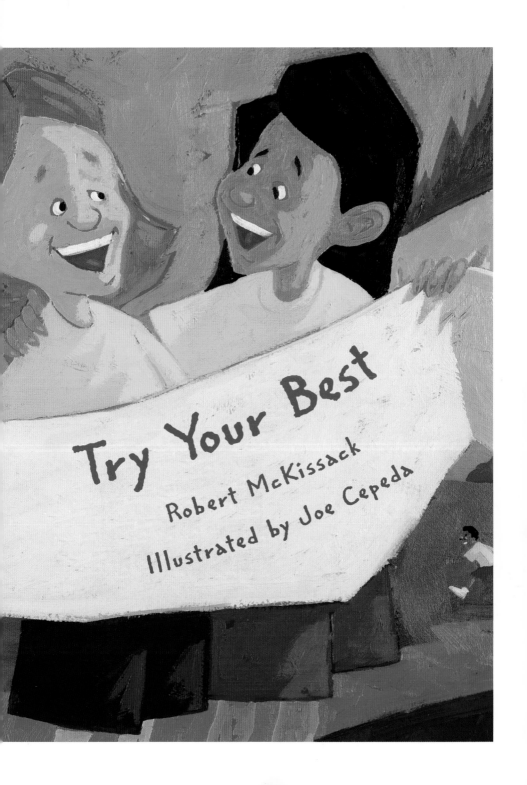

Try Your Best

Robert McKissack

Illustrated by Joe Cepeda

"It's Sports Day," said Mr. York.
"Oh, good!" said Jan.

"Oh, no," said Ann. "I don't think I'm very good at sports."

"Just try your best," said Mr. York.
"Let's start with soccer. Kick the
ball, Ann!"

"Oh, no," said Ann.
"Just try your best," said Mr. York.

"What a kick!" said Jan.
"You helped us score."

"See, Ann?" said Mr. York.
"You can do it."

"Next you can climb the rope,"
said Mr. York.

"Oh, no," said Ann.
"Just try your best," said Mr. York.

"Good job, Ann!" said Mr. York.
"Now let's run a relay race."

"We need one more to play," said Jan.

"Can you be on our team, Mr. York?"
asked Ann.
"Oh, no," said Mr. York. "I don't
think I can run very fast."

"Just try your best," said Ann.
"You are right, Ann," said Mr. York.
"I'll just try my best!"

Mr. York started to run.
Then he saw a big frog.
He ran very, very fast!

"Run, Mr. York!" called Jan.
"Go, Mr. York!" yelled Ann.

"I did my best!" said Mr. York.
"Yes, Mr. York," said Ann.
"You *and* the frog did your best!"

Think About It

1. Why doesn't Ann want to play on Sports Day?

2. What do both Ann and Mr. York learn?

3. What makes Mr. York run so fast?

4. Do you like the way the story ends? Why or why not?

5. Which of the Sports Day games is your favorite?

I Can Do It
Mobiles

WHAT YOU'LL NEED

 paper

 yarn

scissors

tape

 crayons

 hanger

Cut some circles out of paper. On each circle, write a sentence about something you can do.

2

On the back of each circle, draw a picture to go with your sentence.

3

Use yarn and tape to hang your circles from the hanger.

Share your mobile with a friend. Then do one of your favorite things together!

Meet the Author and Illustrator

Robert McKissack thought about his childhood summer camp when he wrote *Try Your Best*. Some of the other kids at camp were afraid to try new things, and they missed out on all the fun. He thinks everyone should try their best. "Reach for the stars," he says. "You may go there someday!"

Joe Cepeda loves to imagine pictures in his mind. He also watches his son play with other children because it gives him ideas for even more pictures. He says, "I like to think of my work as a celebration of color, shape, and people." He hopes you have fun reading this story!

Requests for permission to make copies of any part of the work should be mailed to the following address: Permissions Department, Harcourt, Inc., 6277 Sea Harbor Drive, Orlando, Florida 32887-6777.

www.HarcourtBooks.com

First Green Light Readers edition 2004
Green Light Readers is a trademark of Harcourt, Inc., registered in the United States of America and/or other jurisdictions.

Library of Congress Cataloging-in-Publication Data
McKissack, Robert L.
Try your best/Robert McKissack; illustrated by Joe Cepeda.
p. cm.
"Green Light Readers."
Summary: When Ann worries that she is not good enough to participate in Sports Day, her teacher encourages her to try her best.
[1. Sports—Fiction. 2. Teachers—Fiction. 3. Schools—Fiction.
4. Self-confidence—Fiction.] I. Cepeda, Joe, ill. II. Title.
III. Series: Green Light Reader.
PZ7.M478695Tr 2004
[E]—dc22   2003012868
ISBN 0-15-205089-2
ISBN 0-15-205090-6 pb

A C E G H F D B
A C E G H F D B (pb)

Ages 5–7
Grades: 1–2
Guided Reading Level: I
Reading Recovery Level: 15

Green Light Readers
For the reader who's ready to GO!

"A must-have for any family with a beginning reader."—*Boston Sunday Herald*

"You can't go wrong with adding several copies of these terrific books to your beginning-to-read collection."—*School Library Journal*

"A winner for the beginner."—*Booklist*

Five Tips to Help Your Child Become a Great Reader

1. Get involved. Reading aloud to and with your child is just as important as encouraging your child to read independently.

2. Be curious. Ask questions about what your child is reading.

3. Make reading fun. Allow your child to pick books on subjects that interest her or him.

4. Words are everywhere—not just in books. Practice reading signs, packages, and cereal boxes with your child.

5. Set a good example. Make sure your child sees YOU reading.

Why Green Light Readers Is the Best Series for Your New Reader

● Created exclusively for beginning readers by some of the biggest and brightest names in children's books

● Reinforces the reading skills your child is learning in school

● Encourages children to read—and finish—books by themselves

● Offers extra enrichment through fun, age-appropriate activities unique to each story

● Incorporates characteristics of the Reading Recovery program used by educators

● Developed with Harcourt School Publishers and credentialed educational consultants

Daniel's Mystery Egg
Alma Flor Ada/G. Brian Karas

Animals on the Go
Jessica Brett/Richard Cowdrey

Marco's Run
Wesley Cartier/Reynold Ruffins

Digger Pig and the Turnip
Caron Lee Cohen/Christopher Denise

Tumbleweed Stew
Susan Stevens Crummel/Janet Stevens

The Chick That Wouldn't Hatch
Claire Daniel/Lisa Campbell Ernst

Splash!
Ariane Dewey/Jose Aruego

Get That Pest!
Erin Douglas/Wong Herbert Yee

Why the Frog Has Big Eyes
Betsy Franco/Joung Un Kim

I Wonder
Tana Hoban

A Bed Full of Cats
Holly Keller

The Fox and the Stork
Gerald McDermott

Try Your Best
Robert McKissack/Joe Cepeda

Boots for Beth
Alex Moran/Lisa Campbell Ernst

Catch Me If You Can!
Bernard Most

The Very Boastful Kangaroo
Bernard Most

Farmers Market
Carmen Parks/Edward Martinez

Shoe Town
Janet Stevens/Susan Stevens Crummel

The Enormous Turnip
Alexei Tolstoy/Scott Goto

Where Do Frogs Come From?
Alex Vern

The Purple Snerd
Rozanne Lanczak Williams/
Mary GrandPré

Did You See Chip?
Wong Herbert Yee/Laura Ovresat

Look for more Green Light Readers wherever books are sold!